CW00858009

(C) copyright to John C Burt words,text and
photographs and drawings 2017.

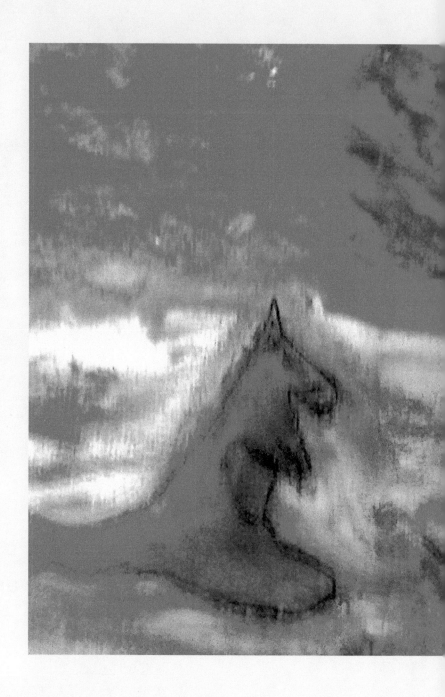

Once upon a time in the Great Southland of Australia, they had a summer to remember of heat, sun, humidity and fire and days of firestorms engulfing the Australian bush.

One particular day a Momma Kangaroo was looking after her joey and had to avoid a firestorm that had been building all day.

The Momma Kangaroo avoided the firestorm by hopping and bounding along the roadway in front of the firestorm with her joey safely in her pouch.

The firestorm was just outside Mudgee in the Central West of New South Wales, Australia. The flames of the firestorm were very high and it took a lot for the kangaroo to escape .

9

The Momma Kangaroo loved her joey very much and she was a very good mother to her child. She was always seeking to protect her joey from the elements, the wind, rain, sunshine and even the odd fire.

Her joey loved her back as well and delighted in sitting in her pouch.

One day all the Kangaroos in the area decided to have a union meeting. The kangaroos of the Great Southland had been unionized fro a long time. There was much to discuss and they had to elect new office bearers for their union. A new President of the union as well a treasurer who could look after their assets.

You may be wondering to yourself what assets the Kangaroo union could have? The assets of their union included the keys to every paddock in the central west and all the way up to the Queensland border. In these paddocks were the grasses that fed the Kangaroos. Also they had knowledge of water -

holes and they also functioned on the land in the central west and all the way up to the state border as fire marshals. They warned human beings of the presence of scrub fires and bush fires as well. In this they functioned much like the Rhino's of Africa. The difference being a Kangaroo would not put a fire out?

All the members of the Kangaroo union movement were the Kangaroo Mamma's there were no male members of the Kangaroo Union Movement. They met every week and had on site union meetings in the paddocks in the area that was closest to most of the members of the union. From time to time the union members would visit cattle stations to assess the

The fire risk to the cattle stations homesteads and the human beings living there. This was a free service the Kangaroo union offered the human owner's of the various stations?

At the particular union meeting on this day there was a rather heated argument about the best paddocks to eat in and the best watering holes and

where they could be found? There was a dull moment at any and every Kangaroo Union Meeting?

The union members all agreed they had to do more to look after their joey's and make sure they provided all they needed. They also agreed that it was getting harder to find a good feed in the paddocks in the central west ?

Some of the members of the Kangaroo union thought that they all should head across the border to Queensland. They had heard the feeding was so much better now in that state. There was now after a lot of rain in summer a lot more grass on the ground and apparently the weather up north was rather pleasant. Also may well be the fire risk would be reduced?

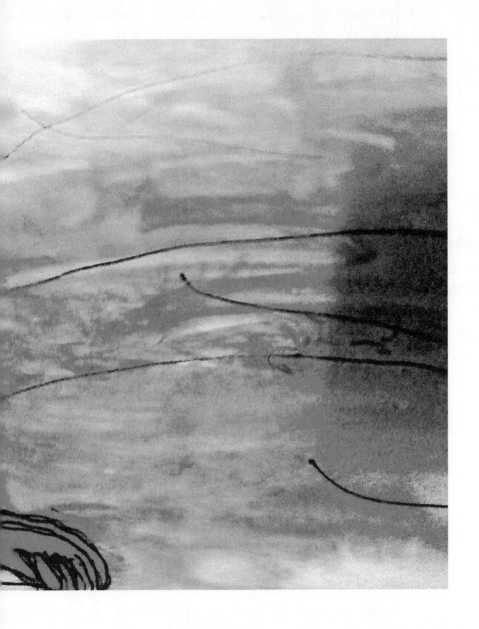

At the union meeting of the Kangaroo's a Kangaroo called Madge was elected as the new President of the Union of Kangaroo's NSW Central West Branch unopposed. Also a Kangaroo named Sally was elected as the new Treasurer also unopposed. So now they had the new office bearers they had to decide whether or not to go to Queensland?

As you can probably imagine this was a very hard decision for the members of the Kangaroo union to make. In the end they decided to remain on duty as fire marshals in the central west of New South Wales Australia ....

For which we are all thankful ....

Lightning Source UK Ltd.
Milton Keynes UK
UKHW021004090619
344059UK00002B/47/P